W9-BDL-757

EASY WORK!
An Old Tale

retold by Eric A. Kimmel

illustrated by Andrew Glass

Holiday House/New York

THE OREGON TRAIL

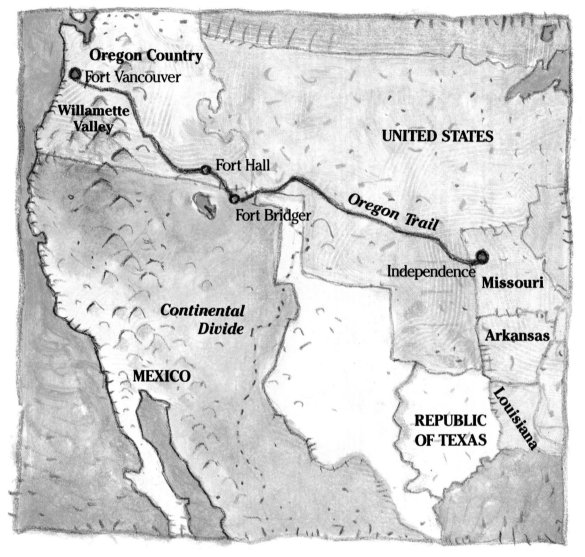

Mr. and Mrs. McTeague came over the Oregon Trail with two oxen, a dog, a cat, and a cow named Abigail. They staked a claim in the Willamette Valley and built their cabin up against the hillside.

Every morning, as soon as the sun came up, Mr. McTeague went off to the woods with the oxen. He worked hard all day, chopping down trees and pulling stumps.

Mrs. McTeague stayed home in the cabin. She worked hard, too. She milked the cow, churned the butter, chopped wood, took care of the baby, spun, wove, sewed, baked, cooked, cleaned, laundered, and saw to the hundred and one chores that go with running a house.

One evening Mr. McTeague came home. "I'm tuckered out," he said as he sat down at the dinner table.

"So am I," said Mrs. McTeague.

"What are you tired for? You don't do anything but sit around the house all day. That's easy work!"

"Is that what you think?" Mrs. McTeague exclaimed. "You should stay home and do what I do. Then you'll know what work really means."

"I'd like to," said Mr. McTeague. "I could use a rest."

"So could I," said Mrs. McTeague.

Mr. and Mrs. McTeague decided to switch jobs. The next morning Mrs. McTeague would go off to the woods. Mr. McTeague would stay home and do the chores.

"Mind what you're doing. I don't want to come home and find a mess," Mrs. McTeague said before she left. "After you milk Abigail, take her up the hillside to graze. Check to make sure she doesn't wander away. Churn the butter, bake the biscuits, and keep your eye on the baby. Think you can handle that?"

"Easy work!" laughed Mr. McTeague.

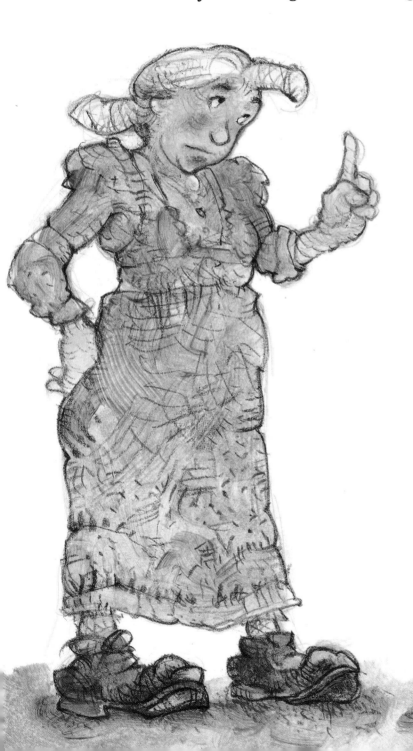

Mrs. McTeague shouldered the ax and led the oxen off to the woods. Mr. McTeague watched from the doorway. "Now what was the first thing I had to do?" he said as soon as Mrs. McTeague was out of sight. "I remember. Milk the cow."

Mr. McTeague carried the pail and the milking stool out to the pasture. He tied Abigail to the fence and began milking her. Suddenly Abigail lifted her leg and kicked the pail over.

"Jumping Jerusalem!" Mr. McTeague exclaimed.

When he bent down to pick up the milking pail, Abigail kicked him over. "You wicked beast!" Mr. McTeague cried. Then he realized what was wrong. "Abigail doesn't recognize me. She's used to being milked by Mrs. McTeague."

Mr. McTeague had a plan. He put on Mrs. McTeague's bonnet and Sunday dress. Sure enough, Abigail thought he was Mrs. McTeague. She let him milk her without any trouble at all. Of course, Mrs. McTeague's Sunday dress got mighty soiled with milk, mud, and cow pies. But Mr. McTeague didn't worry about that.

"Easy work. Nothing to it," he exclaimed.

Now it was time to take the cow up the hillside to graze. "I can't stand around watching her. I have a better idea," Mr. McTeague said. He tied a rope to Abigail's hind leg, let it down through the chimney, and tied it to his ankle. "Now for the chores."

Mr. McTeague mixed up the biscuits, put them in the Dutch oven, and set them to rise. He poured the milk into the churn and started churning. It took longer than he expected. "The butter won't come," Mr. McTeague said. "I'll give it a rest. I know I need one."

Mr. McTeague lay down on the bed and had a nap.

He awoke in time for lunch.

"I'm hungry," said Mr. McTeague. He cut himself six slices of bacon. He put them in the skillet, lit a fire in the hearth, and set them to frying. Then he went back to the churn.

The dog smelled the frying bacon. He wandered into the cabin and lay down on the floor, wagging his tail back and forth. The cat came in, too. She settled herself beside the churn, hoping for a few drops of milk.

Suddenly the baby began crying. "Holy Hannah!" cried Mr. McTeague. "I can't churn the butter, fry the bacon, bake the biscuits, and rock the cradle, too!"

Just then he had an idea. He tied the cradle to the dog's tail. Then he sliced some more bacon and cut it into little pieces. He threw the pieces to the dog one by one. The dog wagged his tail, the tail rocked the cradle, and the baby fell asleep.

"Easy work!" said Mr. McTeague, feeling proud of himself. He went back to the churn, but the butter still wouldn't come.

"There must be a better way," said Mr. McTeague. Suddenly he had another idea. He got out the flour barrel, turned it on its end, and set a chair on top of it. Then he got out his banjo, climbed onto the barrel, sat himself down in the chair, and tied the end of the churn to his leg with another piece of rope. Mr. McTeague started picking his banjo and singing,

"Oh, don't you remember Sweet Betsy from Pike,
Who crossed the wide prairie with her lover Ike…"

He kept time with his foot. As his leg moved up and down, so did the handle of the churn. After each song, Mr. McTeague threw a piece of bacon to the dog. The dog wagged his tail, the cradle rocked back and forth, the churn went up and down, the bacon sizzled in the skillet, the biscuits rose in the Dutch oven, Abigail grazed on the hillside, while Mr. McTeague sat on top of the flour barrel, playing the banjo, and having a gay old time.

"Easy work! Nothing to it!" said Mr. McTeague. He even made up a song that he sang to the tune of Little Brown Jug.

"I work my fingers to the bone.
Mother sits at home alone.
Loafs around the livelong day.
Mighty easy work, I say.

"Ha, ha, ha! I do say,
Woman's work is child's play.
Ha, ha, ha! I can see
That's the kind of work for me!"

But the butter still wouldn't come. Mr. McTeague began to get sleepy. His head drooped forward, and soon he was snoring. That's when the trouble started.

The bacon grease in the skillet caught fire. The dog began barking and woke up the baby. The baby began screaming and woke up the cat. The cat began yowling and woke up Mr. McTeague, who opened his eyes to find the back wall of the cabin ablaze. "Golly Neds!" he yelped.

He grabbed for the water bucket to put out the fire. Unfortunately, he forgot he was sitting on top of the flour barrel, tied to the churn. Over went the barrel! Over went the churn! Over went Mr. McTeague!

The dog saw his chance. He grabbed the whole slab of bacon and ran out the door, dragging the cradle behind him.

"The baby!" cried Mr. McTeague. Covered with flour and dripping milk, still wearing Mrs. McTeague's bonnet and Sunday dress, with the churn tied to his leg, he took off after the dog. When the dog saw this terrifying apparition coming after him, he dropped the bacon and ran up the hillside, still dragging the cradle, with the poor frightened baby screaming her head off.

The dog ran straight for the cow.

The cow took fright and bolted over the hill as fast as she could go. Unfortunately, the rope on her hind leg was still tied to Mr. McTeague's ankle. As Abigail ran, she dragged Mr. McTeague back into the burning cabin, through the milk and flour . . .

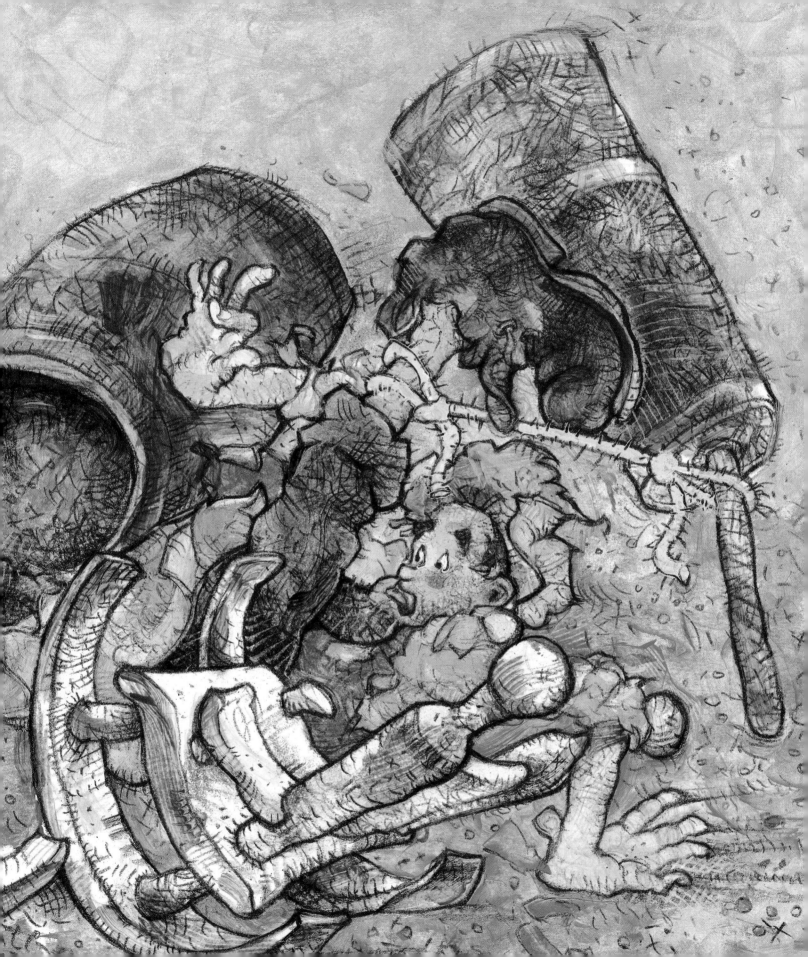

... through the sizzling bacon grease, over the Dutch oven, across the ashes, up the chimney, up and over the top of the hill.

Mrs. McTeague came home from a hard day's work in the woods. She had cut down trees, pulled stumps, burned brush. It was hard work, but not much harder than what she was used to. She came home expecting to find supper on the table. Instead, she found:

The cabin burned to the ground.

The baby covered with dirt, crying in her broken cradle.

The cat lapping up the last of the milk.

The dog gnawing the last of the bacon.

The cow gone.

And Mr. McTeague, dressed in the ragged remains of Mrs. McTeague's bonnet and Sunday dress. His hair and beard were singed off, and he was covered from the top of his head to the heels of his boots with flour, curdled milk, bacon grease, biscuit dough, ashes, soot, mud, grass, leaves, twigs, and poison ivy.

"Easy work, eh?" said Mrs. McTeague.

Mr. McTeague had nothing to say.

Mr. and Mrs. McTeague built a new cabin. Abigail came home, and eventually everything was set to rights. Mrs. McTeague continued taking care of the house, while Mr. McTeague saw to plowing, planting, and clearing the land. It was hard work, all right, but not nearly as dangerous as housework.

"Easy work?" laughed Mrs. McTeague.

Mr. McTeague shook his head. "Not hardly!"

Author's Note

The story of what happens when husband and wife exchange chores is found in many cultures. An anecdote in the life of Abigail Scott Duniway inspired me to write this version. Mrs. Duniway was a tireless champion of women's rights and one of Oregon's leading suffragettes.

Mrs. Duniway was riding in a stagecoach, returning home from a speaking trip. Among the passengers was a farmer who had indulged in quite a few sips of whiskey. He kept saying to Mrs. Duniway, "My wife doesn't need anything from you. I take good care of her. The little woman hardly has to work at all. She's home right now, toasting her tootsies by the fire." On and on he went, repeating over and over, "toasting her tootsies by the fire." Mrs. Duniway said nothing.

The stagecoach rounded a bend and stopped to let the farmer off. Everyone in the coach could see the farmer's wife standing in front of their house, splitting firewood with a heavy ax. "Ah!" Mrs. Duniway exclaimed. "I see the little woman now, toasting her tootsies by the fire."

The farmer got off without a word.

To Diane, Brenda, and Marianne
E.A.K.

To Caterina and Rebecca
A.G.

Text copyright © 1998 by Eric A. Kimmel
Illustrations copyright © 1998 by Andrew Glass
ALL RIGHTS RESERVED
Printed in the United States of America
FIRST EDITION

Library of Congress Cataloging-in-Publication Data
Kimmel, Eric A.
Easy work!: an old tale / retold by Eric A. Kimmel; illustrated
by Andrew Glass. — 1st ed.
p.   cm.
Based on P.C. Asbjørnsen's *Manden som skulde stelle hjemme.*
Summary: Thinking his work in the fields is harder than his wife's
work in the house, Mr. McTeague trades places with her for one day.
ISBN 0-8234-1349-7 (hardcover)
[1. Folklore—Norway.]   I. Glass, Andrew, 1949–   ill.
II. Asbjørnsen, Peter Christen, 1812–1885. *Manden som skulde stelle*
hjemme. English.   III. Title.
PZ8.1.K567Eas   1998   97-28184   CIP   AC
398.2′09481′02—dc21
[B]